Cici #3
A Fairy's Tale

A PERFECT VIEW

Written by
Cori Doerrfeld

Illustrated by
**Tyler Page and
Cori Doerrfeld**

GRAPHIC UNIVERSE™ • MINNEAPOLIS

Graphic Universe™ is a trademark of Lerner Publishing Group, Inc.

Graphic Universe™
A division of Lerner Publishing Group, Inc.
241 First Avenue North
Minneapolis, MN 55401 USA

For reading levels and more information, look up this title at www.lernerbooks.com.

Main body text set in CCDaveGibbonsLower 10/11.
Typeface provided by ComicCraft.

Library of Congress Cataloging-in-Publication Data

Names: Doerrfeld, Cori, author, illustrator. | Page, Tyler, 1976– illustrator.
Title: A Perfect View / written by Cori Doerrfeld ; illustrated by Tyler Page and Cori
    Doerrfeld.
Description: Minneapolis : Graphic Universe, [2017] | Series: Cici: a fairy's tale ; 3 |
    Summary: "While camping, Cici finds out that she experiences nature differently
    as a fairy, which turns all her plans upside-down" –Provided by publisher.
Identifiers: LCCN 2015044432 | ISBN 9781467761543 (lb : alk. paper) |
    ISBN 9781512430684 (pbk.) | ISBN 9781512427004 (eb pdf)
Subjects: LCSH: Graphic novels. | CYAC: Graphic novels. | Fairies–Fiction. | Magic–
    Fiction. | Camping–Fiction. | Hispanic Americans–Fiction.
Classification: LCC PZ7.7.D634 Pe 2017 | DDC 741.5/973–dc23

LC record available at https://lccn.loc.gov/2015044432

Manufactured in the United States of America
1-37129-18117-4/13/2016

For Erin

—C.D.

17

About the Author and Illustrator

Cori Doerrfeld is a freelance author and illustrator who holds degrees from St. Olaf College and the Minneapolis College of Art and Design. She has written and illustrated several picture books, including *Penny Loves Pink, Little Bunny Foo Foo: The Real Story, Matilda in the Middle,* and *Maggie and Wendel.* She lives in Minneapolis with her comic artist husband, Tyler Page, and their two children, Charlotte and Leo. You can follow Cori's work on her website: www.coridoerrfeld.com.

Tyler Page is an Eisner-nominated and Xeric Grant–winning artist and educator. In addition to publishing his own work, he illustrated the *Graphic Universe* series *Chicagoland Detective Agency* and has created comics and illustrations for a variety of commercial clients. He is also the director of Print Technology Services at the Minneapolis College of Art and Design. He lives in Minneapolis with his wife, author/illustrator Cori Doerrfeld, and their two children.